© **Ewan Rilad 2022.**

To Elaine, with amusement.

EARLY LIFE

Hi, I'm Bobby the Wolf and back in the early fifties I was the leader of West Ham's Inter City Firm, and one of the most feared football hooligans of the day. Later on, I became an underworld enforcer and by the time I was twenty-seven, I had risen high in the criminal underworld serving as chief henchman for London crime boss Percy Boston until his untimely murder in 1952.

Indeed, some of you may have heard about me and will know I enforced his authority by beating up and stabbing people; and in one case burning alive somebody who had got in his way and refused to pay a debt. While others will know of the occasion I buried a grass who was passing information to the police, and got most of the mob locked up in the process. Hurting and maiming people was what I liked to do and was born to do.

    I was born on the 8th December 1932 in Stratford, East London not far from the Royal Docks where my father, Harold Wolf worked as an electrician and my mother, Virginia Wolf (no not the writer), was employed as a part-time cleaner. I lived at Number 2, Sandy Close, which was a two-minute walk from Upton Park the home of West Ham United, and every Saturday when West Ham was playing you could hear the roar of the crowds as they urged their team on.

Most of the time, the only thing you could hear was West Ham supporters yelling, "Come on you Hammers," but occasionally you could hear the away fans chanting, and when you did it was usually a sign that their team was winning and West Ham was losing.

I was too young to attend matches at this early stage of my life, but my father always went to them as indeed did my granddad, which was hardly surprising because both had been West Ham supporters all their lives (the club had been going since 1895) and they had lived and breathed West Ham for years, as had many who lived in the area.

I know most people's memories of life before they started school are somewhat vague and consist mainly of being pushed around in a pram or attending large family get-togethers, and to some degree so were mine. However, the thing I remember the most was not one or other of these two things, but of lying in my cot or playing out in the garden as yells of, "West Ham we love you..." filled the air.

When I was five, I was enrolled at the nearest Catholic school, which was St Anne's, on Stanley Street given both my parents were Catholic and I had already been baptised into the Catholic faith.

It was September 1938 and the countdown to World War Two had already begun with Hitler marching into the Sudetenland and British Prime Minister Neville Chamberlain returning from a meeting with Hitler shortly afterwards waving an agreement promising, "Peace in our time," which was not worth the paper it was written on.

   Still, I couldn't have given a damn about that, what five year old could. We were too busy settling into our new schools and making new friends. Some of the kids I already knew because either they lived in the same street as me, or, our dads went drinking together and I knew them that way. Kids like Johnny Gregson for example, or Albert Cookson and Jimmy Wheeler, but others I didn't know like Roy Gotman, Frankie Parker, and Harold Stinton, but who nonetheless became part of my inner circle.

In fact they became part of my gang and I say my gang because I quickly established myself as their leader. It wasn't hard because I was the most charismatic, and I was the best fighter of all of them, as Frankie Parker discovered to his cost when he stepped out of line one day in the yard.

What happened was I accidently banged into him when we were playing football during the dinner break and instead of just shaking it off he got all gobby and started having a go. So I punched him in the gob and left him in no doubt who the boss was.

Another kid who needed to be taught a lesson was Brian Thompson. He was older than I was and slightly bigger than me, which was something because although I was only five years old and had just started school, I was far bigger and broader than most kids in my school let alone my year. It therefore makes you wonder why Thompson was stupid enough to target me in the first place.

Anyway, the altercation began when Thompson, who was leaning against the school railings at home time with his mates, called me over and demanded I steal some sweets from Heatons on the corner for him.

I smiled wryly. I had seen Thompson pulling this stunt before with the new kids and knew it would be my turn soon so I was ready for it.

"Yeah," I cried. "In fact I have some sweets for ya now... let me give them to you." I fumbled about in my pockets for a few seconds before pulling out a pair of knuckledusters and hitting him so hard he hit the deck looking somewhat bug-eyed as he did.

His mates were looking on in surprise too, and I was ready to punch any of them who came near me but I was grabbed from behind by the headmaster, Mr Jenkins, and told to report to his office in the morning.

"Certainly sir," I said, before stepping forward and punching Thompson again as he tried to get to his feet. "See you then."

The following morning I was in for a shock, because I had thought all I would get was a telling off as I did at home when my parents were upset with me. That was not to be. This was 1930's England and kids were taught discipline or it had to be installed into them more harshly. So, once I had reported to Mr Jenkins's office, he frogmarched me to the front of the school assembly and made me stand there with my hands on my head, which I soon discovered he did with every kid who misbehaved.

Then, when songs had been sung, prayers had been said and the assembly was almost over, he called upon all those, including me, who were standing with their hands on their heads to step forward and bend down. When we did he slashed our backsides so hard with a cane that we virtually flew through the roof before crashing down and bursting into tears.

I was fuming, particularly when I saw Thompson standing at the back of the assembly hall grinning from ear to ear, and I thought there was no way I was going to let it pass, not by a long shot.

So, at home time I was waiting for him in the woods behind the corner shop because I knew that once he had bullied some kid into stealing sweets for him that is where he would go to eat them because he always did. The minute Thompson saw me standing there with a machete in my hand, and my teeth curled back in a snarl, he legged it, as did his mates, and it was very lucky for them I did not catch up with any of them and lay into them. If I had done, I would have chopped off their fucking heads and stuck them on poles for all to see, and trust me, I wasn't joking. Not fucking joking at all.

The following day I was ready to confront Thompson and his goons again, but I was in for a pleasant surprise. Although they were waiting for me at the school gates it turned out they weren't there to harm me but to try and get on my good side. Thompson, in particular, went out of his way to be ingratiating, which was hardly surprising given I had chased him with a machete the previous day hoping to chop his head off now was it.

    If some lunatic had chased me with a knife, I wouldn't have tried to get in their good books, I would have gone home, got my hands on my father's shotgun, which he used for hunting wild rabbits in the woods on the edge of town, and then gone looking for the little bastard and blown his fucking head off with it. But, Thompson as I said was very eager to please and this became clear the minute I got near the school gate.

"Hey Bobby," he cried, when he saw me coming up to him. "How you doing?"

"Never mind how I am," I said with a growl. "I have something for you."

I pulled out the machete I had had with me the previous day and his eyes nearly popped out of his head.

"No no, Bobby," he said, fumbling about in his pocket and pulling out a bag of sweets. "I'm not here to fight you ... I'm here to give you these. They're lemon sherbets and they're your favourite I understand. I'm sorry for all the trouble I have given you, we all aren't we lads?"

He looked at his mob for support and they all nodded nervously, before turning back to me and saying, "and it won't happen again. We won't treat you with such disrespect again."

"Damn right you won't," I said putting the machete away and grabbing the sweets, "because next time you do I won't be so lenient and I really will chop all of your fucking heads off."

They gasped.

"Oh and another thing," I said, taking a lemon sherbet out of my bag and fixing them with a firm stare. "I want you to give me a bag of these every day when I arrive at school, just to show you are not lying and really do respect me."

"What?" Thompson was puzzled. "How do I do that? Those things are damn expensive."

I glared at him. "Get one of the younger kids to rob them like you tried to get me to," I said as he stared at me with a baffled expression. "What the fuck do you think you do?"

With that I walked off leaving them all staring after me with looks of pure horror on their faces.

After that, I settled down at the school and had no further problems from anyone. Even Jenkins, the headmaster, seemed wary of upsetting me because whenever he caught me bullying one of the other kids into doing my homework or nicking something I wanted down at the market, which I did on a regular basis, he did nothing other than go pale and walk away.

I guess it was because he had got it into his head that when the brake cables of his car snapped causing him to skid and do himself an injury, it was me who had tampered with them. Not only did it take place shortly after he had caned me, but at a time when word was spreading that anybody who did me an injury would very quickly suffer one of their own.

Still, he never said anything and I settled down to life at the school easily enough and it seemed like no time before I had moved into my second year and a notch up the food chain so to speak. But, as I said before, the countdown to World War Two had already begun when I had started school a year earlier and now on my first day back at school it began in earnest when Hitler invaded Poland and the whole British Empire was at war with Germany.

I must admit I was quite excited when hostilities broke out because the thought of people killing each other and shooting at each other was rather appealing. I can remember most vividly sitting at home with my parents and grandparents as Mr Chamberlain announced on the radio that we were at war with Germany.

Then, things took an unexpected turn because the government

decided in their wisdom that because of concerns that the Germans were about to bomb London and other major cities, it would be advisable if kids were evacuated to different parts of the country and as quickly as possible. The scheme was voluntary and no kid could be evacuated unless their parents gave their express permission, which unfortunately for me, mine did.

I couldn't believe it. I really couldn't and I kept saying to my mother, "Why Mummy? Why do I have to go?"

"It's for your own sake son, that's why," she said gently stroking my hair. "We don't want you getting killed if the Germans do bomb the city."

Well I yelled and screamed and threw a couple of wobblies, but it did me no good and on the day of my evacuation she took me down to the station where all the other kids who were being evacuated were and I quickly spotted Mr Jenkins amongst them. He was walking around and trying to ease the concerns of both kids and parents.

After he had spoken to my mother I was put on a train and as it pulled away and my mother was waving at me tearfully, I yelled over to Mr Jenkins who was standing waving everybody off.

"Do you realise that if this war lasts two years I will be too old to come back to your school and you may never see or hear from me again?"

He just nodded and said, "I do Bobby I do."

I lost sight of him for a few seconds after that because the smoke from the train rose and blocked my view, but after it had gone I spotted him again and he was grinning. I swear to God you would have thought by the way he was grinning that the man was pleased to see me go, and the mere thought that he may never see me again, was just too much for him ... he was clearly finding it hard not to throw his hands in the air and do cartwheels to celebrate the fact.

Once I settled down on the train and looked out of the window, I felt as though I was in a whole new world. I had never been out of my hometown before and knew nothing about London other than the narrow confines of Stratford, and its familiar landmarks. But now as those landmarks disappeared and the train roared through London, they were replaced by new landmarks and places I knew nothing about and I must say I found the whole thing rather enthralling.

    I sat with Johnny Gregson and Albert Cookson whose parents had also agreed to the evacuation and we just stared out of the window, saying, "Cor look at the funny old building,", "Cor look at that odd shaped house," or, "Cor, look at that fancy car that man is driving." It was a fantastic experience and although I was only six years old, I fell in love with trains and developed a love of railways that would stay with me for the rest of my life.

Evacuating so many children was a huge logistical exercise that required not only teachers, railway staff, and the police, but also local authority officials, a number of which had accompanied us on the train, headed up by a weedy looking man called Fisher. He was a barrel of laughs I must say. I don't know what it is about government officials, particularly council ones, but no matter how high up or low down the greasy ladder they are, they all seem to think they are something special and give themselves airs and graces, when in reality they are nothing more than a bunch of pen pushers.

That is precisely what Fisher was doing and it didn't take me long to upset him. When I asked him how it was he had managed to arrange for himself and his buddies to have tea and sandwiches on the train, but he had not managed to arrange it for us evacuees, he became apoplectic with rage and I felt sure he was going to give me a clip round the ear. But, something in the way I was looking at him told him that would be a very silly thing to do, a very silly thing to do indeed. Instead, he just stormed out of the carriage and that was the last I saw of him.

Well that was until we got to Euston anyway, when he suddenly reappeared on the platform and started fussing about like an old hen.

Because the government had issued parents with a detailed list of items their children should bring with them when they were being evacuated, most of us were carrying a suitcase containing underclothes, slippers, nightclothes, spare socks (or stockings if female), a toothbrush, comb, towel, soap, facecloth, handkerchiefs and a warm coat, as well as a gas mask in case the Germans started bombing the city as we were in the process of being evacuated.

There were some exceptions to this, as some of the kids came from very poor families and couldn't afford to provide some or any of the items listed. I include my good friend Albert Cookson, whose parents were drunken layabouts, in that. I can always remember him telling me many years later, that the reason his parents had agreed to allow him to be evacuated wasn't for concerns about his safety, but so they wouldn't have to spend money feeding him and instead would have more money to spend down at their local boozer. I must say this was very callous of them don't you think?

A few minutes later, we were all put into the care of the women from the Women's Voluntary Service (or WVS as they were known) and after we had said our goodbyes to Fisher and the rest of the council officials who had accompanied us, we were led away to a platform on the other side of the station.

The WVS were volunteers whose 17,000 members provided practical assistance to tired and apprehensive evacuees at railway stations and provided them with tea and refreshments. I was delighted when they took us into a billeting hall, or reception area as they were also known in those days, and given a hot cup of tea along with sandwiches and a piece of chocolate, because I was famished. I couldn't eat them fast enough. I ate them so fast that I had finished mine by the time Albert and Johnny had only just begun theirs.

I said to them, "Stay here while I go and get some more grub because I am still hungry."

I tried to get more, but the stupid woman at the counter where the food was being dished out wouldn't give me any, because, like Fisher, she was a pompous swine and full of her own self-importance. I stormed out of the reception area and onto the platform to steady my nerves and to stop me thumping her.

Outside on the station, the weather had turned cold and I heard somebody with a cockney accent say to another geezer with a goatee beard, "Well Bill, with this weather I doubt Adolph will send his bombers over tonight."

Then I heard the sound of laughter behind me and when I turned round I was amazed to see a little girl standing there and grinning like a Cheshire cat.

"What the hell are you grinning at?" I asked, looking her up and down and thinking what a strange looking creature she was with her pointed nose and hair tied back in a ponytail.

"I'm laughing at you," she cried, "and the way you stormed out of that room just now, when you didn't get what you wanted."

"Oh you are, are you?" I was amused by her forthrightness. "Who the hell are you?"

"I'm Barbara," she replied, "and you?"

"I'm Bobby Wolf."

"Bobby Wolf," she burst out laughing. "You mean you're named after the Big Bad Wolf in Little Red Riding Hood?"

"Yes, I suppose, I am," I cried, laughing despite the absurdity of it, "and I suppose you are little Red Riding Hood herself?"

"Oh no," she replied grinning. "I'm your fairy godmother which is why I am giving you these." As quick as a flash she handed me some sandwiches and a bunch of chocolate bars and I stared at her in surprise.

"Where the hell did you get them from?" I asked, grabbing them from her and quickly stuffing the chocolate bars into my pocket.

"Nicked them, didn't I."

"You nicked them?" I said surprised.

"Yeah, when you were storming out the reception area and everybody was looking on, I took the opportunity to nick them."

I laughed and just then the girl's mother appeared, took her by the hands, and led her away. My lasting memory of her was her looking back at me with a slight twinkle in her eye and a cheeky grin on her face.

CLOVELLY

About an hour later, I discovered that the WVS didn't just provide tea and refreshment for young evacuees, but also hosted them in their own homes and treated them like members of their own family.

The first I knew about it was when a group of them took me, along with the rest of the kids from my school, to one side and told us we would be going to stay with them at their homes in Clovelly, which we were told was a small village off the West Devonshire coast.

We were gobsmacked when we heard this because up until then none of us had known where we were going, because neither Mr Jenkins nor any of the local authority officials had been able to tell us. This was mainly because they themselves didn't know. But none of us expected to find ourselves being taken to a village which none of us had ever heard of, in a county which none of us had ever been to, and which was hundreds of miles away from our homes at that.

However, at least we weren't going to a castle on one of those godforsaken islands off the Scottish coast or to some unpronounceable place in Wales as kids from other schools were, and for that I was eternally grateful.

I can't say I remember much about the train journey itself because I fell asleep as soon as I sat down and didn't wake up until I got there, which meant I had been asleep for the approximately seven and a half hours that our journey had taken.

Once we got there, we were told to get off the train and stand in line while our names were read out. When they were, we had to pick up our suitcase and go home with whoever had called out our name.

I was one of the last to be called and when I was, I discovered to my horror that I would be staying with the same lady who had refused to give me more sandwiches back in London when I had asked for more. I could see by her face that she was just as shocked and surprised to see me. Still, she led me out of the station and over to her house, which was nearby. After letting me in and closing the door behind her she proceeded to tell me her name was Mrs Williams and that we would be living here by ourselves, as her son had been called up for the war, and her husband had died many years earlier. She had a tear in her eye when she said that, but quickly pulled herself together, before giving me a homily on what I could and could not do.

I won't go into the ins and outs of what that entailed, but basically it meant being a good boy and doing what she said when she said it.

"You will be a good boy, young man won't you?" she said, looking at me with a stern expression.

"I'll try to be Mrs Williams," I said, "but the problem with that is that sometimes I can be a naughty boy, a very naughty boy indeed."

With that I sat down on my bed and invited her to join me. We didn't have intercourse, I was far too young for that, just kissed and cuddled and stroked each other's hair.

You would not have guessed anything was going on, if you saw us outside in the garden or whenever she took me to my new school, because when she did our behaviour was no different to that of anyone else's.

Indeed, like all child evacuees we had to attend school, because school didn't stop just because there was a war on, and I was enrolled at

Clovelly Juniors along with Johnny Gregson and all the other kids from the East End who had been bussed here with me.

It wasn't long before I got into trouble. The local kids didn't like us upstarts coming to their school and invading their territory and it wasn't long before a 'them and us attitude' prevailed, with them sitting on one side of the class, and us on the other side, and them taking their meals on one set of tables and us on another.

But the real friction came outside in the playground, as you might expect, because that's where most fights break out at school.

One particular fight began after one of the local kids, a big fat dollop called Peter Trefelis, decided to trip

Albert Cookson up as he was walking past him sending him tumbling to the ground where he banged his head causing him to suffer a bout of concussion.

Trefelis thought it was funny when Albert was taken inside for medical treatment as did all his mates, but they weren't laughing when I went over and chinned him sending him tumbling to the ground and needing medical attention himself. In fact they were looking extremely gobsmacked, particularly when I told them that if any other evacuees, or me, experienced any more problems from them, then they too would be needing medical treatment and when I said medical treatment I meant medical treatment ... like treatment for a wound caused by a baseball bat to their face for example.

After that I had no problems with any of the kids at that school. In fact barriers came down and we all became good friends and like most kids we used to spend our spare time fishing or watching the trains go past on the way to Plymouth or wherever they were heading. We also used to sit in Mrs William's back room listening to the radio and how the war was progressing as the logs burned in the sizzling fire. I was seven when I heard about Dunkirk and eight when I heard Hitler had gained mastery over Europe, but then the stupid bastard went and invaded the Soviet Union before declaring war on America. How he thought he could take them on as well as us at the same time is anybody's guess.

By the time I was ten years old, we had received the news that we had defeated the Germans at El Alamein and by the time I was eleven the radio had blurted out victories at Midway, Stalingrad, and Normandy. But it was when I turned 12 and heard that the allies had entered Berlin, and Hitler had shot himself dead, that we cheered the most. Once everybody had gone home I took Mrs Williams upstairs and undressed her before losing my virginity in a night of fun.

RENT PROBLEM

As it happened, the Japanese surrendered not long afterwards and with it the war came to an end. I was delighted, but not for long as my mum and dad were killed a little while later when some drunken bozo in a lorry went and crashed into the back of the taxi they were travelling in killing them, my grandparents, and the driver instantly.

I couldn't believe it ... I really couldn't. I mean they had survived the war, the Blitz, the V2 bombing etc., and now they had been killed and all because some bozo had had one drink too many. It was unbelievable it really was, and I desperately wanted to blow his fucking head off, but he had been killed in the crash too.

Still the death of my parents did leave me with a problem because it meant I was now an orphan and it raised the question of where I was going to live now the war was over and kids were returning home to their families.

At first social services thought it might be a good idea to ship me off to Australia, to begin a new life, as many kids who found themselves orphaned after the war were, but that didn't work out because there were no ships sailing at the time and I didn't want to go anyway.

Another option was to put me into a children's home and let Barnardo's take care of me, but I didn't want to go into a kids' home and Mrs Williams who I had been staying with while these shenanigans had been taking place didn't want me to either. So, she applied to adopt me and I can't say I was surprised because she had not only been my legal guardian during the war but also my lover and neither of us wanted that relationship to end.

In fact, both of us were determined it didn't because we enjoyed the sex but also the secrecy behind it. Indeed, one of the things that always amused us was how we deceived everybody around us. To the people of Clovelly we were just a normal household; with nothing improper going on behind closed doors. However, behind the scenes it was very different. Behind the scenes, this woman was raping me week in and week out and I say raping me because in the eyes of the law that is precisely what she was doing what with me being underage and all that.

Still we enjoyed the secrecy and I had to sit there and keep a straight face when she told the adoption board that she loved caring for me, and that I was a boy with great potential and great stamina. "Great stamina," she added with a glint in her eye, "great stamina indeed."

In December 1950, I turned eighteen and as a consequence inherited the money both my parents and grandparents had left me. It was a tidy sum and given I had also inherited their houses; it meant I could now live in London rent-free and with a tidy income ... or so I thought.

A few days after my birthday, I turned up at my parents' house to move in, but the door was opened by a middle-aged woman with a cigarette dangling out of the side of her mouth.

"Who the fuck are you?" I said.

"Who the fuck are you?" She yelled as she glared at me. "I'm the lady who lives here."

I had to laugh at that even though I was shocked she was living there. I was even more shocked by her reaction when I told her I was the owner of the house.

"Ney love," she said with a slight twinkle in her eye, "you're never the owner of the house you're too young for that ... besides I rent this house from Mr Crabtree."

"Mr Crabtree?" I was puzzled.

"Yeah the fella who owns Crabtree Estate Agents over in Rothwell Street."

"Oh he does, does he?"

"Aye love he does. So, if you have any problem with my tenancy you need to discuss it with him."

I opened my mouth to speak, but she just slammed the door in my face and left me in no doubt that the discussion was over. It was the same at my grandparents' old house too, because when I turned up there to move in, I found the place already occupied. Once again, the tenant told me it had been rented to him by the now infamous Mr Crabtree.

I was fuming and once I had dropped my suitcases off in a nearby hotel, I went round to Crabtree's Estate Agents to have a word in the man's ear and find out what the hell he was playing at. I was baffled about how he had come to rent out properties that were not his, but mine, and which up to then I had thought had been lying empty. I was also curious as to how much money he had made from renting them, so I could claim it back with interest.

Mr J Crabtree Estate Agents occupied a large building and the door was opened by a pretty little thing with a lovely smile, who, after enquiring as to the nature of my business, took me into a large room surrounded by fancy furniture and a radiator. The latter was a surprise because in those days few houses, or businesses for that matter, had radiators and it occurred to me that whatever else this Mr Crabtree was; he was certainly a very shrewd businessman because how else could he afford a set up like this.

I was served coffee and cake by another sweet looking thing in a pretty blouse before a rather stern older woman, with the air of an office manager, informed me that Mr Crabtree was ready to see me now. I was led down a corridor passing a group of women typing away as I went.

Inside his office Mr Crabtree wasted no time in introducing himself. He was a slimy looking git, wearing a pinstripe suit, black shiny shoes and a silk shirt and tie. He also had olive coloured skin, jet-black hair, and a long pointed nose, and I suspected he was a Jew. Still, he wasted no time in introducing himself.

"Good afternoon Mr Wolf," he said, holding his hand out and fixing me with a beaming smile. "How do you do?"

I ignored the question and didn't bother to shake his hand. Instead I asked him about my houses and what he thought he was playing at renting them out without my permission.

To my surprise, he didn't bother trying to deny it, but pressed a buzzer and in walked two men. They were clearly heavies whose role was to intimidate me and they stood towering over me with scowls on their faces clearly doing their best to scare me.

So, I pulled out a gun and they backed off pretty sharpish, looking shocked as they did. Crabtree too was looking shocked, as indeed was the stern looking bitch next to him, and I told him to answer my question or I would blow his head off and the heads of everybody else off in the room too.

Well all four looked horrified of course, and the woman burst into tears. Crabtree wasted no time in telling me everything I wanted to know and it was quite an eye opener I can tell you. I won't go into the ins and outs of everything he said because it would take too long, but the gist of it was he was renting my houses out without my permission because he said it was common practice. He said after the war, it was amazing how many empty houses there were and how easy it had been to rent them out.

But I told him that still did not make it legal and he said that he would make me an offer. He said he would pay me part of the rent he collected from my houses, and transfer the money into my account on a monthly basis. He also said he would backdate the deal to when he had first begun renting them out and he even went to his safe and handed me the backdated money in cash.

It was a good deal but I didn't trust the man in the slightest, so I asked him to put it in writing. After he had done so, I left the place a lot happier than when I had entered and with my pocket bulging with wads full of cash.

HOOLIGAN

I wasn't stupid though. It was clear to me that Crabtree was a crook and crooks don't like others showing them up in front of their buddies and getting the better of them, do they?

So, for the next few days I was on my guard. I never went anywhere without carrying a loaded gun, and everywhere I did go I made sure I wasn't being followed and that in itself was quite an ordeal I can tell you. This is because when I was walking down a road I would be scanning all the faces coming towards me, in case I recognised one of Crabtree's heavies, and had to take action to stop them inflicting harm on me. Or if I was in a pub I would be sitting there staring at people as they came through the door in case one of them was there to do me over and I had to move fast.

Nobody ever did and as the money Crabtree promised me from renting both my houses out went into my bank account just as he said it would, I soon started to relax and enjoy life a bit more. I always had a revolver with me in case I needed it though.

A few weeks later I decided to seek out my old mates Johnny Gregson and Albert Cookson, who I hadn't seen since the end of the war when they had returned to their families after the Germans had surrendered.

I didn't know if they were still in London or had moved elsewhere and so I was delighted when I knocked on Johnny's door and his mother told me he was up the road in the Elm Tree with Albert. I quickly made my way over there to see them both. As I approached the pub however, I noticed this dark-haired youth loitering by the door and immediately that our eyes met he glared at me for a few seconds before scurrying into the pub leaving me to wonder what the fuck that was all about.

I didn't have long to wonder though, because as soon as I entered the pub I spotted a group of tough looking youths wearing West Ham shirts and I guessed they were there to watch West Ham play, because the latter was playing at home that day.

But that wasn't what grabbed my attention. What did was the fact they weren't swigging beer and laughing and joking amongst themselves as people do in the pub, but staring at me as though I was a freak from the circus.

So I said, "What the fuck is wrong with you lot?"

The next thing I knew, some lanky bastard had pinned me up against the wall with his hands against my throat and fumes of ale pouring from his mouth.

"Now then you Hull bastard," he growled, giving me another dose of alcoholic fumes as he did, "come to spy on us have you?"

"Spy on you?" I was puzzled.

The lad pulled a wry smile. "Don't try to act all innocent with me," he said. "You're a spotter for Hull City's firm; the Hull City Psychos aren't you?"

"Hull City Psychos," I replied, even more puzzled. "I've never heard of them in my life."

He went to hit me, but then somebody yelled, "Hold on Brian, he's got a Cockney accent so he must be local."

Brain stopped, reluctantly, and I headbutted him so hard he dropped to his knees before I smashed my fist into his lousy gob leaving him flat out on the ground.

His mates were shocked, and some of them came towards me menacingly, but then another voice yelled, "Whoooooa that's Bobby the Wolf, my old schoolmate." I turned round and saw my old mate Johnny Gregson standing next to Albert Cookson with big smiles on their faces. I smiled too and the next thing I knew I was part of a merry group chatting away and having a right old laugh about the good old days.

It was fantastic as many of them had gone to the same school as me, and remembered the punch ups I had had, even though they were a couple of years younger and I didn't know them from Adam. Indeed, we had such a good time that nobody paid any attention to Brian, who was still laying flat out on the floor. But then he suddenly came to his senses and he was helped to his feet. He was very shaken up and confused.

Once I had been told his full name was Brian Hickman and that he was their top boy, I waited for him to recover properly, knowing he would attack me again because I had showed him up in front of his firm. But all of a sudden the same dark-haired youth who I had spotted earlier, came barging in and said the Hull firm had arrived. Before I knew it Brian and the rest of the West Ham mob had dashed outside to confront them but not before Brian had pointed an angry finger at me saying it wasn't over yet and he would deal with me once he had dealt with the Hull City firm.

I stayed inside the pub and watched through the window as Johnny and Albert went steaming into the Hull City Psychos, along with the rest of the West Ham mob. To say it was entertaining was an understatement. Both sides were evenly matched and both traded blow after blow with people going down on both sides, and blood squirting out of the noses of many of those who received a kick to the head or a fist in the face. Johnny was putting up a good show but Albert who couldn't punch a hole in a paper bag, let alone a rival hooligan, was on the floor having his head stamped on. I didn't intervene because it was their fight not mine.

But then the West Ham firm suddenly turned and did a runner and with the Hull City firm in hot pursuit, I decided to follow them because I was curious as to where they were going and what would happen next. To my surprise the West Ham mob turned, and legged it down an alleyway which led to wasteland. Before the Hull firm knew it, they were stuck in the middle of nowhere with more West Ham hooligans waiting to fight them after luring them to this out-of-the-way spot.

I had to admire West Ham for that, but had business of my own to settle so I pulled out a gun and fired it in the air causing both mobs to wheel round and stare at me bug-eyed. I then told all of them to piss off except Brian and fired my gun above their heads to emphasise the point.

Once they were gone I put my gun away and moved towards him with my fists raised and a dangerous glint in my eye, before teaching him a lesson he would never forget. Namely, that Bobby the Wolf was not a man to piss about with, and I mean not to piss about with at all.

Brian Hickman gave me no more problems and I became the top boy of the Upton Town Boot Boys as the West Ham firm were known.

It was quite an eye-opener I can tell you, because up to then I had thought that football hooliganism was a relatively new phenomenon, given I had never heard of it before. However, as it turned out, the history of football hooliganism could be traced back to the 1880s when the football league was formed and with it club rivalries. This is because many of these rivalries were formed off the pitch as well as on it with gangs of rival supporters eager to fight each other and show the other who was boss.

They were the first generation of football hooligans, but unlike their more modern contemporaries they rarely spent their weekends travelling up and down the country to have it out with their rivals because most of them could not afford to do so. Indeed, most of them were employed as factory workers or in other menial jobs where wages were poor and hooligans barely had enough money to feed themselves let alone travel the country to do battle with their rivals.

Another reason was because public travel was not as fast then as it is today. Back then the only way to get from one part of the country to another, apart from walking it of course, was to go by stagecoach, canal barge, or train. Walking was obviously out of the question, as it would take days and even weeks to walk from one part of the country to another, and stagecoaches and barges were not much quicker either. Indeed, the quickest form of travel in those days was the train given there were no planes or automobiles around, and even then trains took longer to reach destinations than they do today. For example, trains from Manchester to London took six hours and not the two hours they do today.

Therefore, most of the earliest fights between rival hooligans were between those who did not have to travel far to engage in their hooligan activities, such as Aston Villa and Wolverhampton Wanderers, Blackburn and Burnley, and Stoke and Derby. This in fact remained the case up to the 1920s when hooligans started to venture further afield as wages improved and public transport became a lot quicker.

The following Saturday, West Ham was playing Luton Town away which meant we were up against their firm, the Luton Town Park Boys. Quite what sort of firm these guys were was anybody's guess. Nobody in our firm had ever come across them before because they had only recently been promoted to league division two. As it happened though, we didn't get to find out because the stupid bozos never showed up. I found out later it was because the night before, they had been out boozing with one of their mates, who was joining the army the next day, and so were too hung-over to turn up.

I was fuming about that on the train back and kept saying what a bunch of wankers they were for wasting our time like that. It was the same when we got back to the Elm Tree pub, but Johnny Gregson lessened the blow by telling me that when a rival firm failed to show up for a fight, it was classed as a victory in the hooligan world, because they hadn't been prepared to fight you.

That was comforting and after I had had a few pints with the lads I went to the phone box across the road to call for a taxi.

But then, a black cab pulled up and this elderly looking geezer said, "Taxi sir?"

I smiled thinking what good timing it was and got in. However, as I plonked myself down in the back seat, the taxi sped away with such speed it sent me wheeling backwards and I cried, "What the fuck!"

Then I saw a rough looking thug who had been crouching down by the front seat. He sprung up and pointing a gun at me, he said, "Relax Mr Wolf and sit back. Our boss would like a word with you..."

With that, I was taken for a ride through the backstreets of London looking down the barrel of a gun as I did so.

PERCY BOSTON

For the next hour or so, I was driven through London with a gun aimed at me by a man who I was in no doubt would use it should the situation warrant it.

Various thoughts raced through my mind as the car scurried down one road after another. Should I try to grab the gun, or make a dash out of the door once it came to a standstill, or should I try to crash the car by punching the driver in the head so I could make my getaway in the confusion? Sounds crazy I know, but when you're in the back of a car with two men you don't know and one of them is pointing a gun at you, it's amazing what thoughts race through your mind.

Indeed, I was still thinking these thoughts when to my astonishment the car turned into a long driveway and pulled up outside a rather lavish house. The man with the gun told me to get out still pointing the gun at me as he did. As I got out of the car I could not help but think that Crabtree must be worth a lot more money than I thought if this house was anything to go by. I had no doubt Crabtree was behind it ... I mean who else could it be? I had not crossed swords with anybody since I had arrived back in London, except that idiot Brian Rickman and he couldn't afford a house like this surely.

As soon as we reached the front door it was opened by a butler and to say I was surprised would be an understatement. I was also surprised when I was led down a very large hallway, containing expensive looking ornaments as well as pictures of battle scenes, which had taken place centuries ago. One of them included a soldier brandishing a large sword about to hack off the head of a fellow soldier during the War of the Roses. I wondered if the person behind my kidnapping had a similar fate in store for me.

    At the end of the hallway the butler stopped and knocked on the door.

    A voice said, "Come in."

The butler did so with me following behind him and the man with the gun following behind me. I saw Crabtree sitting on one side of a very plush desk, and a man in a pinstriped suit sitting on the other. The latter wasted no time in introducing himself.

"Mr Wolf," he said, getting up and shaking my hand. "How do you do? I'm Percy Boston. I'm very pleased to meet you. Very pleased to meet you indeed."

So that was my first meeting with Percy Boston and it wouldn't be my last. This is because after he had introduced himself he quickly got down to business and told me the reason he had brought me there was because he wanted me to join his firm. He said he was a successful businessman with an interest in a number of ventures including prostitution, gambling and nightclubs, and he reckoned a man like me would be an asset to his business, particularly given the way I had turned the table on Mr Crabtree and his associates by pulling a gun on them when I had visited his office. In fact, he said a man like me would go far in his organisation and he offered me a job there and then at £5 a week, which was real money in those days with the average man earning a lot less.

I of course didn't need the money as I was self-sufficient, what with me inheriting a decent sum from both my parents and grandparents, as well the income I got from renting out their former properties. However, I accepted the job anyway because the man with the gun was still standing behind me and pointing his gun at me as we spoke.

    That said I had no intention of working for him. After I got back to my hotel the plan was to get a good night's sleep or what was left of it as it was now half past one in the morning, before doing a runner back to Clovelly and laying low for a while until Boston had forgotten about me and I could get on with the rest of my life. But then, that damn fool Crabtree went and ruined my plans...

He turned up at my hotel the following morning while I was still in my bed and said he had a job for me. My first thought was to punch him and his two heavies in the face, knock them out, and then do a runner, but it occurred to me that if I did that I might not have two houses left. He would either burn them down or stop transferring the rent he collected on my behalf, until I showed up to collect it... at which point, he would then have me killed for double crossing him, and his boss.

So, I got dressed and once I was in his chauffeur-driven car, he wasted no time in getting down to business. It seemed that amongst his many business interests, Percy

Boston was what was known as a moneylender and it was Crabtree's job to make sure anybody who owed him money paid up on time or suffered the consequences. By that I mean they were either beaten up or else they had property taken from them which covered the debt.

I didn't have a problem with that because I took the view that if somebody had been stupid enough to get into debt then that was their problem not mine. But, I wasn't quite sure why he needed me along for the ride so to speak. I mean he had two heavies with him to handle any rough stuff, so why would he need me there?

It soon became apparent, because he said he wanted me to take over the job of collecting debts. He said it was his job to oversee Mr Boston's interest in our part of London and make sure that everything ran smoothly. This, he said, meant ensuring he had the right people under him to do the jobs that needed to be done and he felt that I would be the right person to handle the debt-collecting side of the business as he knew I was not averse to pulling a gun out on anybody who displeased me.

    I had to laugh at that and had further reason to smile when he handed me the gun that had been taken from me the night before, because it was still loaded. I wondered if I should use it to blow Crabtree's head off, as well as the two heavies, before doing a runner to Clovelly as I had planned to do in the first place, but I didn't. Boston would send a hitman after me, and it wouldn't take them long to find out my connections to Clovelly. In fact, I wouldn't have been surprised if Boston knew about them already because he struck me as that type of man. The type of man who would find out everything about someone before employing the person in his organisation.

So, I put the gun away and stared out of the window thinking I would have to kill the bastards together when I could get them alone. A few minutes later, we pulled up outside a block of council flats and got out. To say the place was an eyesore would be an understatement. There was rubbish and graffiti everywhere and I could not understand how anybody could live in a dump like that. I wasn't surprised that the people who did were the types of people who owed Percy Boston money, because the interest payments on his loans were so huge that only those in the greatest need would take them out ... or would be stupid enough to think they were getting a good deal.

Indeed, to give one example of how extortionate his rates were, anybody who took out a loan of say £10 was expected to pay double that back, and within a month at most. Anybody taking out a similar loan at the bank would have to pay far less than that, and would have a lot longer to pay it. Still, it wasn't my job to reason why they had taken out the loans, only to make sure they paid their debts on time and mete out punishment to those that didn't.

We left the chauffeur in the car, an elderly man by the name of Jenkins, and went over and knocked on the door of the first customer whose debt we were there to collect.

It was opened by a grubby looking geezer with shifty eyes who paid up straight away, as indeed did the old guy with a cigarette dangling permanently from the side of his mouth. This wasn't a surprise as everybody who owed us money knew we were coming and everybody knew we expected the money when we did come. This included the middle-aged woman with the wrinkly face who had resorted to prostitution to pay off her debts and even had the gall to ask if I would like to have sex with her so she could get a discount on her debt. To be honest I wouldn't have minded because she wasn't bad looking for a slapper, but I politely declined the request as I was here to do a job. Besides Crabtree was watching my every move.

    I made about thirty calls that day and nobody defaulted on their debt, nobody but one that was and there is always one isn't there? This particular weasel was in his fifties and tried to spin us some tale that he had just been robbed and therefore could not pay what he owed. I put a gun to his head and told him I would blow his fucking head off if I did not get my money. Surprise, surprise it turned out he had the money after all.

    I was amused by that and so was Crabtree and we were still laughing about it when we got back to the car. But then we were in for a shock. Jenkins, the chauffeur, wasn't there. We looked up and down the street and even popped into the shop on the corner to see if he was in there, but he wasn't. So we went back to the car and waited and waited and waited. But the man did not reappear. Eventually, one of the heavies drove us away with all of us scratching our heads in bewilderment and wondering what the hell had become of the chauffeur.

CARDIFF CITY

We drove over to Percy Boston's house to hand over the money we had collected on his behalf. We were even more mystified about Jenkins' behaviour than we had been when we got in the car. Indeed, the more we thought about it, the more inexplicable it seemed. Jenkins hadn't given us any reason to think he was going to do a disappearing act when we had left him in the car. Quite the contrary in fact, not because he had said anything, but because of his demeanour when we had left him. He just sat in the car and reached for his newspaper as he often did when he was waiting for his boss to return.

Various explanations were put forward as to what had become of him as we drove over to Boston's house – from the downright bizarre to the downright sinister. One of the heavies who was with us for example, and whose name was Richardson, was of the view the man had been enticed away by a prostitute while we had been collecting debts. While his friend and fellow heavy, a tough-looking geezer by the name of Fisher, was of the view he had been kidnapped. He pointed out that Mr Boston had made a lot of enemies in recent months after taking over territory which had previously belonged to other criminal gangs and one of them may have kidnapped Jenkins in revenge.

To be honest both were plausible as Boston admitted when we got to his house and told him what had happened. As it was Friday however, and late, Boston said the best plan was to wait until Monday to see if he turned up and take it from there.

I was pleased about that as I didn't want to work over the weekend as West Ham was playing Cardiff away. I wanted to lead our firm into battle and show the Cardiff mob that West Ham was not a firm to piss about with. This may seem strange to you given I was now a gangster and had enough excitement in my life, but for me, hooliganism was a way of relaxing and getting away from the pressures of working for a mobster five days a week, fifty two weeks a year.

To be honest, it was no different to what the football hooligans in the 1920s and 1930s had done. They had held down good jobs in the City etc., but were still hooligans at the weekend because they saw it as a means of unwinding. They included people such as Mad Mark Melechett, for example, who ran with Charlton Athletic's firm the B Mob and was a solicitor by profession, or Dave Doggy Patterson who was an office manager with Bristol Council and ran with Bristol Rovers firm, the Gas Hit Squad during the weekends.

So, I went home to get a good night's sleep but with the uncomfortable feeling that there was more to Jenkins' disappearance than met the eye.

The next morning, I found myself at Euston Station waiting to catch the train to Cardiff and freezing my balls off as I did. It was half past six in the morning and I was so tired, cold, and hungry that I really did wonder why I had bothered to become a football hooligan in the first place. I say hungry because I had left it too long to get out of my pit and I didn't have time to scoff down some breakfast before I came.

Still I didn't have long to wait for the train and in no time at all I found myself sitting in a third-class carriage heading westwards towards the beautiful country of Wales. Most of our firm came from poor working areas of East London and therefore could not afford to travel in a more luxurious style, including my old mates Johnny Gregson and Albert Cookson, who spent most of their time swigging beer with the rest of the firm as I slept and tried to catch up with my beauty sleep.

In fact I slept so well that I was fully awake and raring to go when the train pulled into Cardiff ... but I was in for a disappointment. We had been hoping the Cardiff mob would be waiting for us when we arrived but they were nowhere in sight. I say waiting for us, because this was the

1950s and back then most firms travelled to away games by trains, because it was the cheapest and quickest way to do so. All football firms knew this and would wait for their rivals at the stations.

So, because most of us still hadn't had our breakfasts, we piled into one of those cafes where they do all-day breakfasts and were soon doing justice to excellent bacon and eggs.

About an hour later, I finished my breakfast and looked around me anxiously. I was hoping the Cardiff mob would have arrived by now but they were nowhere to be seen, and I was worried that they weren't going to show up, just as the Luton mob hadn't bothered to show up when we had gone up there to have it out with them a few weeks earlier.

I was also worried that I hadn't seen any of their spotters while I had been eating. If a firm did not show up to have it out with you at the station, then the chances were they would send their spotters down to find you so they could go and have it out with you there and then. Sadly however, they were nowhere to be seen. That said; I couldn't be sure their spotters hadn't seen us even though we hadn't seen them … they may well have done so and reported our whereabouts to the Cardiff mob who might be waiting for us once we walked out of the station or further on up the road. We would have to be on our guard.

As it happened though, they weren't there. But, some of our mob had been to Cardiff before when West Ham and Cardiff had met during a previous encounter, and knew where their local boozer was. So, we headed over there to have it out with them or to trash the place if they weren't.

As we turned into the road where their pub was located however, we saw a bunch of kids sitting on bikes, talking amongst themselves, smoking cigarettes or swigging beer and we knew they were spotters. Spotters were often teenage kids, aged between 13 and 15, who took on the role of spotters because they liked hanging around hooligan firms or because their older brothers were members.

Any doubt about who they were, was soon dispelled when one of them, upon seeing us, flung his bike down and dashed into the pub to let the Cardiff mob know we had arrived, nearly falling flat on his face as he did.

We had to laugh at that and in no time at all the Cardiff firm had stormed out of their boozer and were laying into us with fists flying in all directions. I had to give them ten out of ten because normally when a firm runs out of the pub they square up to their rivals for a few seconds before steaming into them. Today, however, they just steamed straight into us and I was impressed.

That of course did not stop me and the rest of my firm giving as good as we got and in no time at all we were trading blow after blow, kick after kick, head butt after head butt, and smack after smack with me in the thick of it and leading by example, as every top boy should. Indeed, I hit one Cardiff bozo so hard in the gob, that he hit the deck and was out for the count as indeed was another who got in my way ... and then another, and then another. I then jumped up and down on their heads for good measure.

It was fun and I was really enjoying myself but then I heard some bozo yell, "Who's your top boy? Where is he?"

When I looked round I saw some huge bastard, around the same height as me standing there with his fists clenched and ready to lunge forward.

I yelled over to him, "I am. I am West Ham's top boy. I am Bobby the Wolf."

Well God knows what happened then, but before I knew it the bastard had kicked me so hard in the balls I flew through the air and landed writhing in pain. Now I don't care who you are, but if you're a football hooligan and regularly fight rival thugs as all hooligans do – because that's what being a football hooligan means, getting into gang fights with rival thugs – then at some point or another you are going to wind up on the floor writhing in pain or out for the count. That is true of top boys such as me as much as it is for anybody else in a gang.

You wouldn't think so though, if you read books by such notorious hooligans as Jackson Frane and Mickey Crane. If you read their books you may well come to believe that some hooligans never lost a fight, never wound up lying on the floor covered in blood, or never lost out to a rival firm. It was all bullshit because they did and the only reason they didn't admit it is because their egos were too big, and would not let them.

Well mine wasn't and as I continued to writhe in agony the fighting around me raged on. It occurred to me that Cardiff's top boy had done well to put me out of action albeit temporarily, because it not only provided a morale booster to his firm, but also had shaken my own mob up, and put them on the defensive. In fact they were beginning to back off slowly. This didn't surprise me because whenever any top boy is down, it isn't long before the rest of his firm either join him or do a runner. Sensing they were just about to do that, I quickly sprung to my feet and pulled my gun out before blasting it into the air.

Everybody flinched and glared at me as though I was mad including my own mob. That didn't worry me. What did was the fact their top boy had injured my pride and showed me up in front of my mob, and I couldn't allow that because if I did I would lose the respect of my firm and no top boy can ever abide that. So, I went over to their top boy who was whimpering like a dog and thinking I was going to blast his head off and I ordered him down a secluded alleyway at the barrel of a gun along with the rest of his firm. I then got two of my firm to hold him down while I proceeded to rape the bastard as everybody looked on in astonishment including my own firm.

CHAINSAW CHARLIE

On the train home the mood was sombre. Nobody could quite believe that I had raped Cardiff's top boy and everybody was shell-shocked including Johnny and Albert. I wasn't surprised by this because they had known me since childhood and had no idea I was gay.

In fact, I wasn't sure I was gay myself up until then, because although I had always fancied members of my own sex, I had never let my sexual urges get the better of me and had sex with any of them. Quite why that was I couldn't say because it was obvious I was as gay as a kite. However, if push came to shove I would have to say it was because I was getting all the sex I needed from Mrs Williams and therefore had no need to have sex with anyone else and my homosexual urges had been suppressed.

Still, she was in Clovelly and I was living in London so I suppose not having her around to control my homosexual feelings meant they had finally got the better of me and before I knew it I had raped Cardiff's top boy and had done so in front of his firm as well as mine. I wasn't worried by that or even embarrassed by it, because I had actually enjoyed it and found the whole thing exciting. But I sensed that some of the lads might not take kindly to the fact I was gay, if not all of them, so I told them straight that I was gay and asked if any of them had a problem with it.

None of them did, which was very wise on their part because if they had had a problem, I would have thrown those that did head first out of the window. I took the view that gay or not, I was still top boy of this firm and what I said went and God help anybody who thought otherwise and I mean God help them.

The following Monday, I went to Crabtree Estate Agents to find out what jobs he had in store for me that day and to ascertain if Jenkins had turned up after doing a vanishing act the following Friday.

I thought it strange that Crabtree was running his criminal affairs from there, given the large number of office staff he had in the building who could report him to the police if they came across anything untoward. However, I soon found out that they were just as bent as he was. Actually it was quite a clever ploy on his part because if for any reason trouble reared its ugly head, he had lots staff on hand to help him deal with the matter if indeed help was needed.

Still Jenkins hadn't turned up for work and in a way he was very wise not to do so because if he had he may well have been sampling hospital food for a week. This is because Crabtree had told me to do him over if he did not have a good explanation as to why he had disappeared and left us all in the lurch.

I had to find him of course before I could do that and as I could not drive, Crabtree appointed Richardson to act as my chauffeur, with Fisher to provide extra muscle if it was needed. Personally, I didn't think it would be, as I thought it highly unlikely that Jenkins would cut up rough. He did not strike me as the type to use violence if he did not get his way, but in the criminal world you never knew. It is not always the hardest people you have to fear, but the meekest because when they feel threatened or are pissed off they won't hesitate to shoot you, or poison your tea and bury you under a house as was the case with Mrs Crippen. So, perhaps it was best I had back up just in case things got out of hand.

At Jenkins' digs, his landlady was just as puzzled as we were by his disappearance as he had lodged with her for 12 years and she had never known him go away without telling her first. The mystery deepened still further because when she showed us his room we saw that all of his clothes were still there, as was his passport and suitcase. It was further evidence that his disappearance was not planned but perhaps something more sinister.

We then went to check his local boozer and bookmakers to see if he was there and finding he wasn't and had not been in over the weekend either, we reported back to Crabtree that we could not find him and had no idea what had become of him.

Crabtree was disappointed of course and agreed that Fisher may have been right when he had suggested to us the other day that Jenkins might have been kidnapped by one of the criminal gangs whose territory Mr Boston had taken over in recent months. If that was the case then we might have gang warfare on our hands, so Crabtree said he would have to consult with Boston first to see what he wanted doing about it.

While he went off to ring him, we nipped across the road to the cafe to have some dinner. I was famished after what I could only describe as a rather tiring morning's work ... and I mean famished.

About half an hour later, we had finished our dinner and were smoking cigarettes and debating which gang was responsible for Jenkins disappearance and what Boston was going to do about it. I said what he was going to do about it but there was never any doubt about that, because if you mess with a criminal kingpin like Boston, there are only two ways they are going to deal with it. Either they will arrange for you to be put in intensive care, or they will arrange for you to be put in a coffin.

The problem was we didn't know what gang was behind it, or even if Jenkins had been kidnapped at all.

For all we knew, he may well have run off with a married woman. Sounds strange I know, but such things do happen as regular readers of the newspapers will tell you.

Still, that was Boston's problem not mine as Crabtree made clear when I returned to his office to see what he wanted me to do next. Indeed, his precise words were, "Carry on with your debt collecting duties. Boston has got other members of the firm to look into Jenkins' disappearance."

I was annoyed by that because it implied others could do a better job than I could, but he was the boss and what he said went.

I spent the rest of the week knocking on doors and making sure people paid their dues and punching those who did not want to. It was interesting work and the following Saturday I found myself in the Elm Tree pub along with the rest of the West Ham mob as we were playing Blackburn at home that day, which meant we would be up against their firm the Mill Hill Mob.

    To be honest we weren't expecting these bozos to put up much of a fight, because when we had met them on previous occasions they had simply legged it when they saw us coming. But what did surprise me was the number of West Ham hooligans who turned up to fight the Blackburn mob. After I had raped Cardiff's top boy the previous week, I had figured that some of them would not have wanted anything to do with a queer like me. However, they were all there ... including Johnny Gregson and Albert Cookson.

I sent spotters out to locate the Blackburn firm and while we waited for them to report back, I whiled away the time by telling the rest of my mob how I intended to rape Blackburn's top boy if I got my hands on him today. I had had a good few hard days at work, and needed to unwind just like everybody else who had had a hard week at work needed to.

As it happened though, it wasn't one of our spotters who located the Blackburn firm but one of the landlords of a nearby pub. He phoned the Elm Tree pub to say they were in his pub ... making a nuisance of themselves. They were also boasting that they were going to do us over when they came across us.

I had to laugh at that and the fact the landlord had phoned to tell us where the Blackburn mob were because he wasn't doing it out of kindness but necessity. He was doing it because he had been warned that if we ever found out there had been rival hooligans in his pub and he had not rung to let us know, we would smash up his pub and him with it.

The other landlords in our area had been given the same warning too.

Having landlords ringing us was an effective way of locating our opponents other than having our spotters doing it. It prevented them from having their pubs trashed and them spending a month in hospital, and we got to find out where our opponents were even before our spotters did.

So, I sent one of the kids who was loitering outside to go and tell the Blackburn firm to meet us at Gibson's Alleyway and to show them the way there because I doubted very much they would know it themselves unless they had been there before.

Sure enough it worked and when I saw the Blackburn mob I laughed because there were just seven of them and fifty of us. How their top boy expected to take us on with such a pitiful turn out I could not say. Neither could I say why they had decided to follow our spotter down the alleyway because it was an obvious trap. However, they did and it wasn't long before they were cornered with half the lads and me in front of them, and Johnny Gregson and the rest of the lads behind them.

The leader was a big bastard, bigger than I was and just as bulky, which is how I liked them. He was also scowling at me.

I said to him with an odd glint in my eye, "Well now, who do we have here? A right big boy and no mistake."

He looked surprised, "Who the fuck are you?"

"I'm the man who is going to rape you," I replied

"Rape me?" He was shocked.

His mates looked shocked too, but I just pulled out a shotgun and told him to take off his clothes and bend over the bin lying close by.

He stared at me in disbelief for a few seconds and then curled his lips back into a grin. "Certainly," he said, before pulling out a gun of his own and blasting it above my head, sending me tumbling to the ground and dropping my shotgun in the process. "Now, how about I have some fun myself and chop off your head?" he said, before taking out a huge knife and telling me to bend over the bin so he could do it.

Fucking hell, I hadn't expected that and I gasped as did the rest of my firm. The bastard with the knife just smiled down at me and I quickly fumbled about in my coat before pulling out another gun and holding it to his head.

This time it was his turn to gasp, but he still had a gun in his hand and held it to my head before I had time to blink.

It surprised me and for the next few moments we just stood there pointing guns at each other's heads as our respective firms looked on. With each of us pointing guns to the other's head it was clear that we had reached a stalemate and neither of us were prepared to back down. That said; neither of us wanted to die either, so neither of us were prepared to pull the trigger first out of fear the other would shoot back as they hit the deck. We continued to point our guns at each other as all around us hooligans on both sides watched in trepidation.

After what seemed like a lifetime I said, "You're not going to budge are you?"

He smiled. "And neither are you, are you?"

"Not in the slightest," I replied with a grin.

He smiled and I stared at him. This guy was a pure psychopath. I could see it in his eyes. He knew I was too, because he could see it in mine. So we continued to hold guns to each other's heads before I said with a frown, "Who are you anyway?"

"Charlie McFudden," he said proudly. "And you?"

"Bobby the Wolf," I replied with equal pride.

We continued to point our guns at each other until the sound of police sirens filled the air, and before we knew it we were both backing away from each other before turning and leaving it at that.

STUPID BASTARDS SQUAD

To be honest, I was a bit shaken up by that encounter as indeed were the rest of my firm. It just never occurred to me that a rival hooligan would be packing a gun and be as psychotic as I was.

I could not get him out of my head and over the next few days I toyed with the idea of going up to Blackburn to put a bullet in Charlie McFudden's head for showing me up in front of my firm ... but I didn't. For one thing I was too busy with my debt-collecting duties during the week to be able to do that, and for another, I could not get up there during the weekend because of my football hooligan activities.

Now I know it may seem strange that I would be more concerned with engaging with my hooligan activities than blowing the head off some mad bastard who had humiliated me, but when you are top boy of a firm you are expected to lead your troops into battle, week in and week out, come rain or shine.

Another reason however, was that Percy Boston had forbidden it. When you are a member of a criminal firm you need the permission of your boss to kill somebody, no matter how insignificant that somebody is and Boston said no. He said McFudden almost certainly had criminal links of some description, what with him being quite prepared to use a gun and a knife so readily, and he did not want his friends taking exception to me killing him and starting a gang war.

To be honest I could well understand that, because there was nothing more difficult than being at war with a gang that was based hundreds of miles from you, and which you knew very little about, not least because you didn't know who they were and how dangerous they were. Yes, I know the same can be said about football hooligans, but the difference between football hooligans and criminal gangs run by crime lords like Percy Boston is that the former only fight on match days and generally don't go round killing each other, and doing things like burning businesses down ... and criminal gangs do.

So, I didn't shoot up to Blackburn to put a bullet in McFudden's head as much as I wanted to and as much as he deserved it, and Mr McFudden should consider himself very lucky I didn't.

Over the next few weeks, we had run-ins with firms from all over the country including the Aldershot A Company, the Norwich Hit Squad, and the Chesterfield Bastard Squad. Why they called themselves the 'Bastard Squad' was a mystery to me, but it certainly brought a smile to my face. It also struck me that the

Chesterfield mob should be called the Stupid Bastards Squad, because they were one of those firms that got pissed on the way down to London and ended up oversleeping and winding up in Plymouth where they were forced to pay their fares back.

    I did laugh at that but I wasn't really surprised because the number of times I have heard of it happening; of mobs getting drunk on the train and missing their stop is amazing. I blame the railways as much as anybody else, because if they didn't serve alcohol to people when they were already halfway to getting pissed then it would not happen. However, that's just my opinion. You will probably think I am being a killjoy, and that the real blame lies with those bozos stupid enough to get drunk in the first place.

Still, whoever was to blame one thing was certain ... both the Aldershot and Norwich mobs gave us a good run for our money and indeed the Norwich mob sent us fleeing for our lives and putting some of our firm in hospital in the process. I had to give them ten out of ten for that because we were playing them on our own turf and how they got the better of us is a mystery to me to this day. If nothing else, it was a sign that we were not invincible as much as we thought we were and unlike in other hooligan books I am not going to pretend otherwise in this one.

Indeed, one thing that really annoys me about other hooligan books is the way hooligans often portray themselves as being like Superman who never lost a battle or got beaten in a fight. Trust me they did but they don't tell you that because they don't want to appear weak. A rather foolish stance to take given we all lose battles and fights at some stage of our hooligan days but there you go.

THAILAND

The following week the football season was over and with it the hooligan season. This is because when teams are not playing, hooligans don't have an excuse to get together and engage in a punch up and as such, have to find other things to do with their weekends.

This isn't usually a problem because hooligans like everybody else need time off to recuperate and recharge their batteries, which is why I asked Crabtree for time off so I could recharge mine. To my delight, Crabtree said yes.

A few days later, I found myself lying on a beach in sunny Thailand with Mrs Williams in attendance looking out at the deep blue sea.

Now you might be surprised to hear that Mrs Williams was with me, but remember she had been my lover when I was a kid, and that situation hadn't changed simply because I had moved back to London.

We spent a hell of a lot of time chilling out on the beach, laughing and chatting about the good old days, and of course having sex. It was brilliant hearing about what had been going on in Clovelly ... my old mate Peter Trefelis, for example, was now married with two kids and working on the fishing boats as I had done when I had left school. It was also fun going on boat rides, and enjoying seeing some of the smaller islands that were dotted around Thailand. But what was the most fun was hopping onto a jet ski and gliding over the waves with Mrs Williams sitting with her arms around me, as the sun continued to beat down on the deep blue sea, and knowing that meanwhile the search for Jenkins continued back in London unabated.

Another thing I enjoyed about Thailand was its sex tourism industry. This is because Thailand like Holland is known for its rather liberal attitudes to sex and as such boasts one of the biggest sex industries in the world, bigger than Cambodia, for example, which is known as a pervert's paradise. Indeed, Pattaya in Thailand is known as the biggest brothel in the world, and you only have to go there to see why.

Everywhere you go you will see a girl standing on a street corner beckoning you to have sex with her back at your hotel room. Of course you have to pay for the privilege of doing so, but I'm not knocking them for that because if that is how they want to make a living, then who am I to say otherwise. Indeed, I don't have a problem with people selling their body for sex because paying for sex is as old as time. Anyway, we all need sex don't we? No matter who we are, and what our station in life is.

What I do have a problem with is when people are forced into it or they are under sixteen and therefore below the age of consent. That is child abuse and anybody who abuses a child in my opinion should be strung up at the gallows as a warning to others. Indeed, I would do it myself if I ever found anybody abusing a child. This is somewhat ironic though, because I was here with a woman who had sexually abused me as a child; even though I was the one who had instigated it in the first place. Very ironic indeed.

One thing that I was surprised about was that British newspapers were on sale everywhere in Thailand. I did not expect to find copies of the Daily Mirror here, or anywhere outside of the UK, or any of the other major British tabloids for that matter. Still, there were copies here and I really enjoyed reading them even though they contained old news having taken a day or so to arrive here by airplane.

I particularly enjoyed reading the sporting news and hearing how West Ham were doing on the transfer market, because it was a reminder that the football season was only weeks away ... and with it the hooligan season. That was exciting because it meant I would soon be back to fighting rival hooligan firms and raping any top boy who took my fancy, including that bozo from Cardiff who I had raped already.

Indeed, that made me laugh every time I thought of it and Mrs Williams found it funny as well. She used to say, "Well he shouldn't have been a naughty boy then should he, and he wouldn't have got raped."

Of course she was surprised when I first told her about it because she didn't know I fancied men as well as women, but she didn't hold it against me. She knew I was a sexual deviant as I had seduced her when I was a kid and she loved me for it.

So, we used to sit there laughing about it and wondering how the Cardiff top boy would react the next time our paths crossed.

A week later, I was sitting on the beach reading the Daily Mirror and staring down at it in disbelief. This is because the newspaper was reporting that the head of a local man had been found on the gates of Burnley's football ground and the rest of his body a few streets away behind some derelict building.

"Fucking hell!" was my first thought. I hoped that it wasn't Jenkins' body lying there because if it was then what would it being doing in East Lancashire and in a town hundreds of miles away from his home. As far as I knew he had no connections to the town and neither had Percy Boston. Indeed to my knowledge Boston had never crossed swords with any gang from that neck of the woods or even knew anybody from up there.

Still, it wasn't Jenkins' disembodied corpse lying there but a local man called Damon Kerr, or so the newspaper said as I read further down the page. Indeed, I had to blink when I read that because although I had never met him or had a run in with any of his firm, I knew that Burnley's top boy was called Damon Kerr. When you are a hooligan you get to know the names of fellow hooligans. That said, the newspaper never said the victim was a well-known football hooligan or that he was top boy of Burnley's infamous Suicide Squad and so I wasn't sure if it was the same Damon Kerr or just somebody with the same name.

Even if it was that Damon Kerr, I did not see how his murder could have anything to do with his hooligan activities, because hooligans may be violent but they don't go round chopping off people's heads or even threatening to do so. Well other than that mad bastard Charlie McFudden of course; Blackburn's top boy who had threatened to do just that when our paths crossed a few months back.

All the same, it couldn't have been Mcfudden that had chopped off the victim's head and stuck it on the gates because hooligans don't do that sort of thing, do they? Or at least not in my experience they don't.

LIVERPOOL URCHINS

When I got back to England, I had a final night of sex with Mrs Williams before seeing her off at the train station and reporting back for work at Crabtree's office.

In my absence I discovered that Boston had held a meeting with all the main players of the London underworld, including Albert Dimes and Jack Sprat who ran most of London in the 1930s and who denied having anything to do with Jenkins' disappearance. Now whether or not that was true was another matter, because they were both liars and I would not have trusted them as far as I could throw them. But that was

Boston's problem not mine because my job was simply to collect debts on his behalf and make sure everybody paid them on time and that wasn't always easy I can tell you.

One problem was that many of these people were old and frail so you couldn't beat them up for not paying their debt, through fear they would drop dead on you if you did. This was particularly true if they were in their seventies and eighties. Still, the way to get around this was to take their pension books from them, and then on pension day march them to the post office to draw it before taking half the money from them. This would go on every week until they had paid off their debt. Sounds cruel, I know, but they had to pay their debts like everybody else, and the sooner the better because I didn't want them dropping dead on me from old age before they did, did I.

A second problem was how to deal with single mums who had young kids, because if you beat them up for not paying their debts, they could wind up in hospital and there would be no one to look after the kids. Social services would then get involved and you would have all sorts of do-gooders asking all sorts of questions and creating all sorts of problems with it.

Still, one way to get around this particular problem was to get them a job in one of Boston's brothels during the day when their kids were at school, so they could not only pay their debts but also have money to provide their kids with the nicer things in life. Hopefully, it would keep the social services off our backs at the same time. Indeed it was amazing the number of times I did this and the girl later thanked me afterwards for doing it ... and I mean amazing.

The biggest problem however, was what to do with those bozos who didn't want to pay up and did a runner to avoid having to do so. To be honest I couldn't blame them for that, because the interest on these loans was sky high as I said before and there is no doubt I would have done the same. But I wasn't the one who owed the money they were, and once they had fled the scene it took time, money, and manpower to find them; particularly if it meant paying a bent Civil Servant to do it, and these guys did not come cheap at all.

Still, again, that was Boston's problem, not mine because he was the one who had to pay for them to do so and he wasn't pleased about it I can tell you. Indeed he was furious about it, because some of the people who owed him money had fled to places as far away as Manchester, Newcastle, and Glasgow and they thought they were safe.

As a result, it was not uncommon for them to open their doors late at night and find me standing there with a shotgun in my hand, and my lips curled back in a grin, before I blew their heads off, and left them splat out on the floor for not paying their debts. Not that uncommon at all.

A few weeks later, the football season began and West Ham was playing Liverpool at home.

I was delighted because I was itching to get back into the swing of things and kick the hell out of rival hooligans, which that day meant the Liverpool Urchins. We met up at the Elm Tree as usual and sent spotters out to find them and it wasn't long before one of them had reported back to us that they were on the wasteland behind the pub. They were waiting for us to join them so they could kick the fuck out of us, as their top boy Tommy McFey had told the spotter.

Cheeky bastard, I thought to myself ... we'll see about that and I rushed off to meet them with the rest of the West Ham mob behind me.

Sure enough, McFey was there as was the rest of his firm and the moment I saw him I could tell the man was a bruiser and could handle himself well. He was about the same height as I was and bulging with muscles. In fact he looked like a boxer. Once I had introduced myself as Bobby the Wolf and West Ham's top boy, I asked him if he wanted to fuck with me in a one on one.

He smiled and said he would love nothing more than to do that.

He of course thought I meant a fist fight but that wasn't what I had in mind at all. What I had in mine was sex. I pulled out my gun and blasted it above his head, before getting two of my guys to hold him down while I pulled his trousers down and had my wicked way with him, still clutching my gun in case he or his mates tried to do anything about it.

MISS BARBARA WHIPLASH

For the next few months I was busy fighting hooligan firms up and down the country and showing them that the West Ham Upton Town Boot Boys were back in business, and still a force to be reckoned with.

Indeed, we had some good rucks over the next few weeks and came off best against the likes of Leicester, Swansea, and Bury; although we did come a cropper at Stoke, as well as Preston. Preston surprised me because the latter were not known for having a decent mob or even a mob at all. What's more they beat us on our own turf.

I had to blame Percy Boston for that defeat because it was he who had told me not to take my gun to football matches because he was worried I would be caught with it. As I was a gangland hit man, it could create all sorts of problems for him as well as for me, particularly if the police linked the gun to the people I had murdered. So, without a gun I was unable to pull it out and rape any top boy who tried to get the better of us and as a consequence we suffered a couple of defeats.

Still Boston was right not to let me take my gun on my hooligan trips because if the police did catch me with it, and linked it to the murders I could have got hanged because this was the 1950s and the death sentence was still around in those days. I ended up throwing the gun in the Thames and got on with the business of kicking punching and headbutting any top boy who got in my way instead of raping them at the barrel of a gun. Oh boy did I have fun even though I sometimes came off worst.

Indeed, I had so much fun in those days that I sometimes thought it would be better to change the name of our tasty little firm to the Intercity Firm because we went everywhere by train. So in the end I did and none of my firm objected to me changing the name which was a very wise thing to do don't you think ... a very wise thing indeed.

Then my life suddenly took an unexpected twist when Crabtree called me into his office one day and asked me if I had ever heard of Miss Barbara Whiplash. I hadn't and thinking it was a joke I burst out laughing and said I wouldn't mind doing so given her name and all that it implied.

However, Crabtree was being deadly serious. He said he was asking because she and Boston were due to meet soon to discuss a very important business deal that was going down and he wanted to know what I knew about her.

I had never heard of her and couldn't tell him anything, so he then went on to tell me what he knew. He said she was a mad bitch who ran all of Norfolk with an iron fist and would torture anybody who got in her way, using whips, chains, or any other means at her disposal to do so. He said she was a dominatrix who liked to carry a whip around with her at all times, and that she dressed in a weird cat suit to do it, hence her name Miss Barbara Whiplash. What's more, he said, as I continued to try and keep a straight face at the thought of some woman running Norfolk dressed in a leather uniform with a whip in her hand, she was no ordinary criminal and was a highly intelligent woman. She had a memory like an elephant and could memorise a document simply by staring at it for a few seconds.

Well that might be so, but I wasn't interested in how good her memory was, but her hooligan activities and how she became top girl of Ipswich's Punishment Squad. If males who led their firms were known as top boys then the females who led their firms must be known as top girls; although I had never heard of a top girl before.

Still, when Crabtree described her as weird he wasn't kidding. He told me that on one occasion when Ipswich Town was playing Millwall at home, she had trapped the whole of Millwall's notorious F-Troop in a disused factory, and made them bend down and pull their trousers down behind their ankles, before whipping their backsides for being what she described as naughty boys. On another occasion she had actually overpowered Nottingham Forrest's top boy, Brian O'Shea, before tying him up, gagging him, and then raping him just as I had raped top boys who had crossed my path.

While I could see how being overpowered by a woman, not to mention whipped and raped by them, may be embarrassing to hooligans, who thought they were hard men and not people to piss about with, I could also see how her actions could help recruit new members. This is because, let's face it, a lot of men would pay to have a woman whip and sexually abuse them wouldn't they? And I included myself in that. Yet here was Miss

Whiplash providing her services for free. Yes I could well see how her actions could help firms recruit new members ... I could well see it.

Still on a more serious note it was amazing I had never heard of Miss Whiplash before, given she was infamous amongst football hooligans and everybody in my mob had heard about her, including my old mates Johnny Gregson and Albert Cookson. Indeed, they knew all about her because she had once appeared in the Hooligan News, which was a tatty little news-sheet that provided information on hooligans up and down the country.

The paper had been around since the 1890s when some bright spark had the idea of publishing what football hooligans had been up to, and who the main faces were. It was done more out of fun really, but it quickly proved popular with hooligan leaders up and down the country, who liked nothing more than to see their names, and the word top boy, in it. It was good for their ego and I mean good for their ego.

Still when I asked Albert Cookson and Johnny Gregson why they had not told me about her, or shown me the newspaper article in question, given it was their job to provide me with up-to-date information on all the main players in the hooligan world, their answer was pathetic. They said it was because she was a girl not a boy and they thought I was only interested in boys, what with me being a homosexual and all that. Well of course strictly speaking that wasn't true because I fancied girls as much as boys. I was bisexual and not homosexual, but I didn't push it.

I spent the next few weeks collecting debts on behalf of Boston or doing battle with other hooligan firms up and down the country, including at Newport where we ended up having a right ding-dong in a shopping centre. Members of both of our firms got thrown through some shop windows, but I wasn't one of them. I did enjoy the ruck though and returned to London a happy and content man. Those who had got put through shop windows, including

Albert and Johnny; were now languishing in hospital, which is where I should have put them for not telling me about Miss Barbara Whiplash. I had not done so, because they were old school mates, and I still had a soft spot for them ... what with me being the nice sentimental chap I was.

    Unbeknownst to me, however, I was destined to meet Miss Barbara Whiplash very soon, because the next day Crabtree called me into his office and told me that the meeting between Boston and Miss Whiplash was due to take place that afternoon and in some out-of-the-way spot in Kent. He said the meeting was being held there because neither side wanted to hold it on the other side's turf, in case things got out of hand, and one side found themselves having to fight their rivals on their own turf. I had to laugh at that, because it was exactly the same problems football hooligans had when they had to fight rivals on their own turf. I could understand why Kent was chosen because it was halfway between London and Norfolk, so both sides had to travel the same distance in order to get to their destination.

We went down by car with both Boston, Crabtree and I in the back seat, and two men who I had never met before, but who I discovered were two brothers from Peckham called Liam and Frank Carter, in the front seats. The latter did the driving and as we went Boston made it very clear to us that Miss Whiplash was a woman who would not hesitate to kill us all should the situation demand it. He said we should be prepared to kill her, and any goons with her, if he gave the order for us to do so.

Once there, I had to admit it really was a good location for a meeting. We were in the middle of nowhere, surrounded by trees, and beyond them fields which stretched as far as the eye could see. The only thing between the trees and us on the east side was a canal and as we waited for Miss Whiplash to arrive, I said to Boston that it was a good place to kill somebody here because you could dump their body in the water and nobody would ever know.

He laughed, and was just about to reply when we heard a female voice.

"Oh but you don't have to tell him that Bobby dear. He knows that already because he killed a girl here about a year back. Didn't you Boston?"

I wheeled around and there was a woman standing there in a black uniform, carrying a whip, and wearing a face mask. I knew this was the infamous Miss Barbara Whiplash because of the strange attire she was wearing but I was puzzled as to where she had come from because she seemed to have appeared out of nowhere. I was also puzzled by the fact that she knew my name, and seemed to be addressing me as an old friend. However, before I could ask her how she knew me she continued to address Boston directly.

"In fact you had these two monsters hold her down didn't you Boston?" she said pointing at the Carter brothers. "Then you and Crabtree here raped her and threw her into the canal with her hands handcuffed behind her back. Well two can play at that game."

She raised her right arm and before I knew it two shots rang out and the Carter brothers fell, dead onto the ground. I instinctively went to draw my gun, but before I could do so the woman had a gun to my head and was telling me to be a good boy and I wouldn't get hurt. As she did, men in camouflage emerged from the trees carrying guns and quickly had us surrounded.

"What the hell is going on?" I cried. "And who the hell is this girl you say Mr Boston murdered a year back?"

"Oh that was a friend of mine, Bobby dear," she replied, putting her hand in my jacket and relieving me of my gun, "a very good friend of mine. And I'm so pleased to hear that you had no knowledge of her murder. But then I knew that already, because that nice Mr Jenkins told me so when he came to see me a few months back."

"Jenkins?" I was surprised.

"Oh yes. He told me everything and I mean everything, including about you, and where you were from. The minute he did I knew that my Big Bad Wolf was back in my life again and would one day soon be reunited with his Little Red Riding Hood, I knew it at once."

"Big bad Wolf?" I said puzzled. "My little Red Riding Hood. What the hell are you talking about? I've never met you before in my life. In fact, I had never heard of you until a few weeks ago."

"Oh but how can you say that Bobby dear?"

She then walked up to me and kissed me gently on the lips. "Have you not forgotten the war?"

"The war?" I was puzzled.

"Yes, the war. You were upset because the nice woman in the WVS uniform would not give you any more food, and I was the nice girl who stole sandwiches and chocolate bars and gave them to you when you came outside."

I stared at her in amazement. "That was you ... the girl at the train station with the ponytail, who was grinning at me like a Cheshire cat? The one who referred to me as the Big Bad Wolf and you; my Little Red Riding Hood?"

She smiled. "Ah you remember me now, how lovely."

She kissed me on the lips again and then turned back to Boston and Crabtree with a fury in her eyes that made both them and me flinch, before she turned to her associates and said, "Right, let's get on with it. Undress them."

    I watched in astonishment as a couple of her goons did so before handcuffing them and gagging them so they could not cry out. As they did it, cars moved from behind the trees where they had been hidden, and I was amazed to see a group of women getting out of them and walking over to us; some dressed like waitresses. They placed chairs and a table before us and started to serve tea and sandwiches after Miss Whiplash and I had taken our seats.

    After she had taken a sip of her tea she looked at Boston and Crabtree who were shaking like leaves and clearly trying to say something through the gags.

Although I couldn't make out a word of it, it was obvious they were pleading for their lives and trying to find a way out of the pickle they found themselves in.

Miss Whiplash, however, wasn't the least bit fazed and continued to sip her tea before putting her cup down and saying, "Bobby dear, these monsters raped my friend and so it's only fair they get raped themselves and I am giving you first call on it. I know how much you like to rape naughty boys, particularly when they are top boys of hooligan firms."

I looked at her in astonishment that she knew about all of that before glancing at Boston and Crabtree. I said to her, "Actually, they're not my type. Not my type at all."

Miss Whiplash nodded her head. "You have good taste, very good taste. I mean who would want to have sex with these vermin? I mean look at them. Not exactly God's gift are they? Still let's find somebody who will rape them. Ladies," she cried, addressing the waitresses, "Would you care to rape these two monsters?"

They didn't seem surprised by the question but shook their heads as though the very thought of touching Crabtree and Boston horrified them. So, Miss Whiplash got two of her men to do it, before throwing them in the canal just as they had thrown Miss Whiplash's poor friend into the canal handcuffed and gagged a year earlier.

My lasting memory of them was watching them disappear under the water as Miss Whiplash stood there grinning at them with a glint in her eyes and a general air of amusement about her as though she found the whole thing amusing, very amusing indeed.

NOTE FROM MISS BARBARA WHIPLASH

I'm sorry to inform you all of this, but just a few months later Bobby was murdered in Liverpool and so did not have time to complete his book. He was murdered in revenge for raping Liverpool's top boy, Tommy McFey a year earlier. Tommy has since committed suicide because he could not live with the shame and trauma of it all.

In a way it was ironic that the bastard who killed Bobby did so because Bobby had raped his best friend and held him responsible for his subsequent death, because that is why I killed Boston and Crabtree.

The only difference being they had intentionally killed their victim while Bobby had not.

Still, I am not going to tell you more about Bobby's death, other than to say he was burnt alive in a coffin, because I am writing my own autobiography and you can read all about it there. All I will say is that the bastard who killed him cried like a baby – and I mean, cried like a baby – as he was placed in a coffin, and burnt alive at the crematorium, just as Bobby had been.

RIP Bobby the Wolf.

Printed in Dunstable, United Kingdom